for
Oscar and Olive
Heroes of the Many Moons

The
Amber Moons

Written by

Mike Wall

Oscar you inspired me to write this book

Illustrations by

Sarah Peacock

ISBN: 978-1-3999-4815-9

Printed by Swallowtail Print, Norwich

The Amber Moons
Chapters

Chapter 1

The Weather Bomb

There are many moons in our universe, some have intelligent life while others wait to be discovered. Beyond the moons of Jupiter lay 26 small stars known as the Alphabet Planets. Each star had a letter of the alphabet as its name. Star A was the largest with 750 inhabitants and Star Z the smallest with just 380 Zeds living there. The planets had lived in peace and friendship for as long as anyone could remember.

But everything changed when a freak weather storm surrounded the planets and continued for five days. The sky was dark, thunder shook the ground, lightning raced across the heavens and rain flooded the rivers. Communications were poor, while the conditions were getting worse by the hour. Captain Oscar on Star Z was worried that something terrible was occurring. He scanned the sky then lowered his powerful lunar binoculars with a look of horror on his face. He was an experienced space traveller and had heard stories of storms like this, called Weather Bombs, that could destroy a planet in days.

A Weather Bomb is formed when large cosmic cyclones collide and join together, becoming a violent unnatural weather condition with enormous destructive power. These are rarely seen and usually burn out deep in space. However, its course is unpredictable and any moon caught in its path would face total destruction.

The wind was now a ferocious hurricane, tearing trees from the ground and smashing everything in its path. The rain had turned to hailstones the size of your hand and sheets of lightning scorched the earth endlessly.

Oscar called Red and Polly, Z's space observers, to join him. Scanning the weather tracker they could see the barometer had passed code yellow, the worst storms ever recorded, with a long tail still to come. They looked at each other stunned at what they were seeing.

"*This isn't freak weather,*" Oscar said quietly, "*it's a Weather Bomb and the way the storm is developing we have less than 48 hours before we are all destroyed.*" Speaking with greater urgency he continued, "*Come on, no time to lose, we must alert the leaders of the other moons to what is happening and the dangers we all face.*"

There was panic and disbelief when he informed them and shock when he explained he was abandoning Z, blasting into space with his people and setting course for the Moons of Amber.

Some leaders agreed and quickly made similar preparations. They knew Captain Oscar well and trusted what he said. Others dithered and argued, uncertain what to do, which would prove to be a terrible mistake. The chances of escape were diminishing by the minute.

Working at speed, Captain Oscar and his crew prepared their space transporter, the *Cosmic Explorer,* with the supplies they would need for a long journey. The engines were checked and the space compass set as the *Explorer* rocked on its launch pad, buffeted by the worsening conditions.

The citizens of Z boarded, some with great excitement, others worried about the long journey and the unknown world that awaited them. The experienced space travellers settled in quickly, but for some it was their first journey into the vastness of space and they required help and assurance from the crew. But one thing they all shared was the need to escape from Z, fast.

"We've made good time," Oscar shouted as the cargo hatch slowly closed.

Looking out, he could see the destruction of their moon was near.

Chapter 2

Escape From Z

The engines roared into life and the lights dimmed, as slowly the *Cosmic Explorer* lifted into the air, quickly accelerating away from Z. The ship was surrounded by black cloud while lightning illuminated the hail and chunks of storm debris that clattered against them. The transporter shook violently as it burst through the Alphabet gravity ring and into space beyond. It soon steadied as it cruised away from the Weather Bomb and into the darkness of space.

"Search the radar and send out distress signals to see if any other planets have escaped," ordered Captain Oscar. Red, his flight controller, listened intently across the subspace radio. There was static silence for a few minutes then the radio crackled into life.

"I think I have something," he shouted excitedly.

"This is Captain Olive from Planet O calling from the

bridge of the space transporter *Moonlight. We can see and hear you, we are safe with no damage.*"

"*Thank goodness,*" replied Oscar. "*Good to have you with us, Captain Olive, come alongside, we should keep close formation. Are there signs of any other craft?*"

But before O could reply the radio crackled into life again.

"*G to Z, G to Z,*" an alarmed voice sounded, "*this is Captain Noah calling from the transporter Star Shine. We have just broken through the gravity ring. We are safe but it was a terrifying ride. We will be alongside in a few minutes.*"

"*Welcome Star Shine,*" replied Oscar calmly.

"*Wait,*" interrupted Noah… "*Wait… I can see another ship struggling to escape. I think it's X but I can't make contact and… it looks like their booster engine is damaged. It's difficult to see with the black smoke. X seems to have stopped. Oh no! The port engine is on fire, the ship is spinning out of control, it's falling back into the Weather Bomb, it's disappeared… it's gone… X has gone.*"

There was a stunned silence across the radio waves. They were shocked at the loss of X and the unknown fate of the other alphabet moons. Captain Noah joined Oscar and Olive in close flight formation.

Eventually the silence ended when a solemn Captain

Oscar ordered they set course Latitude 49 towards the unexplored Moons of Amber.

"Wait" interrupted Noah "Wait... I can see another ship struggling to escape, I think it's X"

Chapter 3

Journey to the Amber Moon

Maintaining an average speed of super warp 6, Captain Oscar calculated the journey should take no more than 40 days, well within the capabilities of the transporters. Each ship carried provisions to last 90 days, and beyond that they must source and grow what was needed from their new home.

The days passed quickly as the crews checked their craft for damage. Luckily, apart from a few large dents and scorching to the outside, everything seemed OK.

A transporter held two mini space probes in its launch bay, a probe could carry three people. It was important these were in good working order because, if a suitable planet were to be found, it would be a probe that attempted the first landing. Captain Olive had volunteered, with Holly and Ben from *Moonlight,* to fly *Astrix1* on this mission of discovery whenever the time came.

A plan had been agreed to be put into action when they reached the Amber Moons. A small planet that might sustain their life form had been identified on Oscar's solar chart. It was to the north and now just one day away. When they arrived, Z would park outside the gravity pull while O and G circled the moon, one east to west, the other north to south. The ship's brief was to scan the moon for life forms, temperature and possible landing sites. They could then decide if it was safe to launch *Asterix1*.

There was a nervous excitement as the time came for Z to close down its motors. The moon in front of them looked peaceful, part in sun, part in a dark amber glow. The *Star Shine* moved slowly towards the east while *Moonlight* slid silently to the north. The adventure had begun.

The first reports were promising as they circled the moon. Noah had seen great areas of forest and a wide mountain range with a large water source flowing down. They had observed some signs of life on the scanner, most probably animals. Olive was very excited as they had detected large lakes, rivers and an area that could be a suitable landing site for the transporters.

Having completed their journey, both ships docked alongside the *Cosmic Explorer*. The leaders agreed *Asterix1* should be launched from *Moonlight* immediately. Their mission, to find a safe landing spot, analyse the air quality, then attempt a short journey outside to gather water samples and test the terrain.

Captain Olive, Holly and Ben were soon seated in the probe. The doors were shut, the burners glowed and *Asterix1* glided silently from the ship, turning quickly in the direction of the Amber Moon. Looking up, Olive could see the three transporters in formation above her.

The probe cut through the gravity ring and moved towards the surface of the planet. Captain Oscar's voice came over the radio.

"Yes we are OK" replied Olive. *"We have found an area to land and we are now commencing touchdown."*

Holly was flying the probe and switched on the retro rockets.

"More retro power," shouted Olive, *"we are approaching too fast."*

Asterix1 shook as the burners fired again, then silence followed by a slight bump, they had landed.

"Well done," said Olive, as Holly switched off the burners.

They looked at each other. What would they discover? Could they build a new life on this moon?

Chapter 4

A New World

The largest of the Amber Moons was surrounded in an orange and red mist, and its rays bathed the smaller moons in a warm light.

Ben had put on his full protection suit before stepping out of the probe into the night, lit only by the amber glow. He checked the landing site then collected soil and air samples.

"It's cold," he said, as he stepped back into the airlock.

The samples were tested, and the air proved to be of good quality with no impurities, which was excellent news. The soil seemed fertile with no traces of harmful substances but would need further testing. They settled down for some rest knowing a journey of discovery lay ahead of them when they entered this new world in the morning.

A warm sun greeted the team as they exited *Asterix1.* It was a good day to explore, Olive thought, as they headed east towards the lake with its wide flat fields. Picking a path through the long yellow grass was slow but this soon changed to bushes and small trees all laden with fruits of different shapes and colours. Samples were collected as they made their way forward.

A warm sun greeted the team as they exited Astrix1. It was a good day to explore thought Olive, as they picked a path through the long yellow grass.

Walking was easier as the team emerged from the trees into fields with a very large lake beyond that shimmered in the sun. It was hot and thankfully there was no need to wear their space helmets as the air was good.

"This is an ideal docking area for the transporters," Holly said.

It was marked on the map they had been sketching during their walk. They couldn't see the other side of the lake but the water was clear with a waterfall cascading down from the hills to the north.

Samples were taken to ensure all the water sources were unpolluted and safe to drink. Soon it was time to return to *Asterix1* and report their findings to Captain Oscar. Olive led a happy team back to the probe, as it had been a successful first exploration.

Tests showed the water quality was A1. Olive shared her news with Noah and Oscar. It was decided two more probes would join *Asterix1* and explore the mountains to the north and forest to the west. Polly and Red would fly with Captain Oscar in *Astro3,* and Kitty, Tom and Captain Noah in *Sky9*. The probes were made ready as they prepared to join Olive and her team on this voyage of exploration.

Chapter 5

Exploration

There was great excitement as the two probes edged out of the launch bay, silently circling the transporters before dipping away towards the planet below. They were soon through the gravity ring picking up the communication beacons Captain Olive had assembled near to *Asterix1.* Kitty would bring *Sky9* down first, and with a flash of retro rocket and a slight judder the probe made a perfect landing. A few minutes later, Red landed *Astro3* in the exact position Olive had marked. They were expert flyers and made difficult landings look easy.

Captain Olive was busy setting up a communications hub, Noah would fly *Sky9* to the mountains and Oscar's destination, in *Astro3,* was the great forest. Both teams would collect samples, sketch maps of the terrain, keep contact with Olive at base and just explore.

Soon Noah and Tom, with Kitty at the controls, were

lifting off, turning slowly before accelerating towards the silver-blue mountain on the horizon. Kitty flew low over the great lake then, gaining altitude, turned north looking for a landing spot on the lower slopes of the mountain.

Sky9 circled twice before Tom shouted, *"There, down there."* He was pointing to a small lake set halfway up a steep slope with an area large enough to land the probe. It looked promising as Kitty gently guided them into position, then with a blast of the retro burner *Sky9* was down.

"Nice landing," Captain Noah said, as they eagerly stepped out of the probe.

There were faint tracks leading up and after a quick look at the lake they followed the steep path, overlooking a beautiful landscape. As the team neared the top of the slope a low roar could be heard getting louder the higher they climbed. Soon the three were standing at the top gazing at a fantastic triple waterfall, and the noise was deafening. The water cascaded down and split into five before disappearing over a rocky ledge.

"Probably runs into the great lake," said Noah.

Leaving the waterfall they scrambled up a stony path. It was a difficult climb with the hot sun beating down.

Finally they reached the top where rocky ground changed quickly into green vegetation and blue grass.

"*This side is sheltered from the strong sun,*" said Kitty, "*with different plants growing here.*"

After a brief rest Noah urged them to go further before they turned back.

They saw flowers unlike anything they had seen before, then near to an overhanging ledge they discovered two caves just large enough to stand up in. Inside, the caves quickly joined together and became one large magical underground lake. The water gleamed lit by a bright shaft of light from above. The sides of the caves had silver streaks giving off a natural glow.

"*What a discovery,*" said Kitty, "*Yes, mark it on the map,*" Noah ordered, "*this would be a good place of safety if ever one was needed. Now we better get back to the probe.*"

"*Hey wait a moment,*" cried Kitty, "*what is this?*" She was pointing to a small hollow in the side of the cave.

"*It looks like animal bones,*" whispered Tom.

"*Yes, big animals,*" she replied.

Then Kitty made a second discovery, as sitting on a ledge, partly hidden, was a wooden figure.

"*It's the shape of a cone,*" she said lifting it down, "*but larger.*" Dusting off the dirt, golden streaks set in the wood appeared, it was a very interesting find.

"Hey wait a moment" cried Kitty "what is this" she was pointing to a small hollow in the side of the cave.

"*We need to get back,*" said Noah urgently, "*we can take it with us, Olive might have some idea what it is.*"

Soon *Sky9* was back in the air. Kitty flew higher to get a good view of the waterfall then swooped down over the lake to see how large it was. She flew over the glistening water before circling back towards base with the water one side and the lower slopes of the mountain on the other. The probe was cruising at half speed giving them time to observe the landscape as they travelled back.

"*Hey wait, turn back,*" shouted Tom, "*I think there was something behind those high trees.*"

Sky9 circled and hovered but there was nothing unusual

to see. Kitty edged sideways and suddenly four caves came into view.

"*Yes, there it is,*" cried Tom.

The caves were carved into the mountain and hidden by the tall trees. Tracks could be seen leading from the caves, and there were signs of digging and lumps of silvery rock scattered around.

"*This needs exploring,*" said Noah ,"*but not today. We must come back tomorrow and find out more.*"

Chapter 6

An Amazing Discovery

Captain Oscar, Red and Polly sat in *Astro3* watching *Sky9* lift off on its mission to the mountains. Seconds later Red turned on the burners and they were away. Their destination was north to the Great Forest that seemed to cover a large area of the planet. Oscar and Polly enjoyed the view as Red skilfully guided the probe on its journey, sometimes high above the forest, then swooping down for a closer look, so close you could see large golden cones on the top branches.

"Time to put her down," suggested Oscar, *"keep your eyes open."*

Polly spotted a clearing among the trees covered in something blue. Red thought it was a good place so Captain Oscar gave the order and they were soon on the ground. Tall blue grass came up to their shoulders as they stood together outside the probe. Giant trees towered above them as they made their way carefully through the grass before entering the forest and stepping into an adventure they could never have imagined.

It wasn't easy struggling through the forest. Large branches had fallen from the trees blocking their path and patches of red weed that stung if they touched you, were dotted around. The tall trees kept much of the sunlight out, so when a break in the trees appeared it was good to step into the sunshine once again. There were many colourful flowers to be seen and it was Polly who made the first amazing discovery as she collected samples from the forest floor.

Next to a very large tree she spied two golden cones, just like the ones they had seen when they flew over the forest earlier. These are good samples, she thought, as she stretched to pick them up, but as she did a silver glint in the grass caught her eye. Looking closer she gasped in surprise and called to Oscar who came running back. She pointed to the circular object partly hidden in the leaves.

Oscar stared wondering what on earth it was, then Red spoke up.

"Don't touch it," he said in an urgent voice, *"I have seen these rings before. If you step on them they will clamp onto your ankle making it impossible to walk. A space traveller from Planet Q brought one back from the Martian Wars, but who made them or what metal they are made of is a mystery."*

This was worrying news, when the planet was scanned by the space transporters there was no sign of intelligent life yet here in the forest was a carefully concealed trap made out of an unknown metal. How did it get here was the question on everyone's mind. Red threw a rock into the trap and it snapped shut gripping the rock between its teeth. Polly picked up the cones and placed them in her sample bag.

The mood had changed with this discovery. Was there other life on this planet, are there more traps? However, they decided to carry on with vigilance and take great care where they trod.

Although the trees gave them shelter from the strong sun it was still hot and uncomfortable as they scrambled on. Captain Oscar pointed out tracks through the grassy patches of forest, possibly made by animals, which were an easier path to follow. It was mid afternoon when Oscar ordered them to take a rest in a clearing with two large rocks in the centre to sit against.

The team were aware that time was moving on.

"Should we continue further into the forest or return to Astro3?" Captain Oscar asked.

But before anyone could answer a low painful moan could be heard from somewhere in the forest. It was a frightening sound as if something was in real distress. The three looked at each other in surprise.

"We must find out where the noise is coming from," said Polly.

They agreed and carefully made their way back into the forest towards the awful hollering. The moaning became louder *"Oh, Oh, Ah,"* it was a sorrowful sound, *"Ah, Oh, Oh."* As quietly as possible they moved nearer and nearer until eventually a clearing with a small rock pool came into view. The moaning had stopped as they stood at its edge. Polly pointed to a large black object huddled up in a ball next to the pool, and as she did it stood up and gave another awful howl.

Red grabbed Polly by the arm, this thing was at least

"As they watched, it suddenly turned and looked straight at them with yellow glaring eyes that peered out of his long black hair."

nine feet tall, and covered in long black hair from its head to its very large feet. Oscar had noticed one arm was dragging on the floor. As they watched, it suddenly turned and looked straight at them with yellow glaring eyes that peered out of its long black hair. It tried to move towards them but its arm held it back and with another painful howl it collapsed onto the grass.

Polly stepped further into the clearing and waved to the others.

"Come on, it's injured, we must do what we can to help this poor creature."

Chapter 7

The Drag Pod

"*Careful,*" murmured Red, as he and Captain Oscar followed Polly into the clearing.

They stopped a few feet from the creature that was still on the ground, and moaning. Polly took another step forward and touched it gently on the leg. It raised its head, looked at her, and gave out a roar that forced them back.

Without hesitation she moved forward again, this time touching it on the arm.

It let out another mighty roar but Polly didn't step back, instead she looked into its face putting one arm across her eyes. The creature seemed to understand, this was the intergalactic sign of peace, it grunted and was calmer.

"*Look,*" said Red, "*no wonder it drags its arm, there's one of those traps we found in the forest clamped around its wrist, it must be in terrible pain."*

Polly spoke gently, *"Will you let us help you, please let us help you,"* she pleaded.

Captain Oscar noticed a tear in her eye. How brave she is, he thought.

A few seconds went by and then an astonishing thing happened. The bear-like creature raised its body and stood up struggling with the clamp on its wrist, its yellow eyes wide open, and spoke.

"I am a Drag Pod and can understand many Universal Tongues you speak Earthling. I know what you say but I am trapped with this Alien Ring. How can you possibly help me?"

It then collapsed back to the floor with a long sigh and looked up at Polly.

Red knelt down carefully examining the ring, and he noticed it had cut into the Drag Pod's wrist with a green fluid seeping out. Oscar joined him and pointed to a small hole on the top edge, which looked like it needed some sort of key to release the clamp. They tried a Lunar Knife Red had in his pocket but that didn't work.

"I could return to the probe and bring back the Argon Key," he muttered.

An Argon Key is programmed to open most known

locking systems and all probes held one in case the doors jammed or a burner failed to ignite.

"Yes, that might work," replied Oscar, *"and bring the medical kit, I think we're going to need it."*

It would take two hours to return to *Astro3* and another two back. Red collected the navigation unit and fresh water. Polly contacted Olive at base telling her they would be staying out overnight and not to worry. As she did so, Red disappeared into the forest on his long journey back to the probe. Good luck, she thought, hurry back.

Chapter 8

The Drag Pod's Story

Captain Oscar sat next to the creature while Polly gently bathed its weeping wrist.

"Where are you from, are you here to dig the Silver Rock?" it said, quite unexpectedly. *"No, no,"* replied Oscar, *"we are from the Alphabet Planets that were destroyed by a Weather Bomb. Let me tell you what happened and why we are here."*

The Drag Pod listened intently as Captain Oscar told the story of their escape from the Weather Bomb and the journey to the Amber Moons. The creature nodded, sighed and lay back again.

"What do you eat?" asked Polly.

"I am very hungry," it replied in a pitiful voice. *"I need three Golden Orbs a day to keep well but I haven't eaten since I was trapped in the forest two days ago. The Orbs*

grow high in the trees and I am unable to climb for them or search the forest floor."

Polly put her hand into her bag pulling out the two cones she had collected as samples and offered them to the Drag Pod. It sat up quickly and gobbled them up.

"Tell us about the Drag Pods and this planet," Oscar asked softly.

"We have survived on this planet for many lunar years," it answered, *"more than anyone could remember, caring for the forest and plants that grow here. In return the forest sheltered us from the hot sun and provided us with wild berries and, of course, the Golden Orbs. It is written in the Legends of Drag that a Pod who is brave and protects the forest against all dangers will not die but evolve into a Drag On and travel to the distant Drag Star with Golden Wings. Our Sacred Orb of Life gave the chosen ones the power and courage to make that journey."*

"Time passed peacefully," it continued, *"then the Green Aliens came to dig in the mountains for a rock they called Silver. These beings do not live on a moon but travel through space in a Mother Ship. They take what they want from the weak planets and trade the rock for Martian Gold from others. Every quarter moon they came. At first we were ignored but the work was hard and too heavy for them."*

"One day the Aliens appeared in our forest demanding we dig the rock but we refused. We live in the shade of the trees,

the sun burns our eyes and can kill us. They became very angry and said if we didn't dig the rock they would destroy our forest. Some Drag Pods agreed, hoping to save the forest but within three moons their bodies were damaged and they died painfully in the caves."

"The Aliens are not strong but they have sticks that shoot fire, and we could not defeat them. Some brave Drag Pods did fight but they soon perished. A few of us remained and we hid in the low hills and forest but the Aliens knew we needed the Golden Orbs to survive and they placed traps among the trees to catch us."

"I am the last surviving Drag Pod," it continued after a short silence, *"but I was not brave in the face of danger I did not fight the Green Aliens, and the Orb of Life was lost during our escape to the mountains. So I will not travel to the Drag Star on Golden Wings."*

There was another silence as the Drag Pod hung its head.

"I must die here like many of my friends," it whispered.

"This is a good moon," it continued in a louder voice, *"with water, trees and open fields. Plants grow quickly and the air is good. It would make a fine home for your people BUT you will have to face the Aliens, you must be prepared."*

Captain Oscar and Polly were thoughtful, what a terrible thing to happen to the Drag Pods, but would they be strong enough to face the Aliens when their time came was the question on both their minds.

The Drag Pod spoke again, *"The Rock they seek has many mysterious qualities which I do not understand, and they will fight to have it."*

Sighing loudly it lay down next to Oscar and closed its eyes.

The sun had disappeared and the cold darkness of an amber night engulfed them. A large full moon appeared behind the trees and its beams lit the clearing. An hour ago Red had sent a message he was on his way back with the key and medical bag. Not long now, thought Polly, as she pushed her cold hands into the pockets of her thermal suit.

The Drag Pod lay still while Captain Oscar, with his eyes closed, mulled over the amazing story this creature had told them.

Chapter 9

Red Returns

Polly and Oscar were close to sleep and it was a shock when Red stumbled into the clearing with the medical kit over his shoulder. He was late as it had been difficult finding the way back through the dark forest. Red took the Argon Key from his pocket and handed it to Oscar. The Drag Pod sat up and watched as Oscar held the key over the ring, just above the key port. The Argon glowed.

"Good," said Oscar, *"we're ready."*

Polly held her Solar Torch closer as Oscar pushed Argon gently into the key port turning it to the right and then to the left. Nothing, nothing happened, the ring remained locked on the Pod's wrist. Red wanted to try and he eased the key both ways, twice, but the ring stayed shut. This wasn't what they expected.

Polly was getting anxious so she handed Red her torch,

pushed him aside, and pulled the key out. It was covered in green fluid from the Drag Pod's wound. She wiped it clean on her trousers and examined the lock. It was filled with the same green mess. Polly was motionless for a moment, then taking a mouthful of water from her bottle she blew it into the key port, and green liquid seeped out. She did it again with an even larger mouthful, and her cheeks puffed out as she blew the water forcefully into the lock.

"That's better," Polly muttered as she pushed the Argon Key back into the port and turned it. But again nothing moved and the ring remained shut.

With eyes narrowed, she eased the key the opposite way as far as it would go. They sat staring at the trap, nobody dared breath, then a long hissing noise came from the ring, then silence. They looked at each other puzzled, suddenly another shorter hiss sounded and the trap sprang open releasing the Drag Pod from its cruel grip.

The Drag Pod was the first to move, slipping its hand out of the ring then leaping up, it jumped around the clearing bellowing loudly.

"I'm free I'm free, whoopee I'm free."

It hollered and roared with yellow eyes glowing in the moonlight. It was a frightening sight, nine feet tall with long black hair and large feet. They needed to tend the wound and when it eventually calmed down Polly bathed its wrist and Red applied a medical poly tort firmly over the deep cut. Then to their surprise it stood up and announced it was hungry and needed to search the forest for Golden Orbs.

"You are true friends," it said loudly, *"I hope you stay on this moon and we can live together peacefully."*

The Pod patted Polly gently on the head then turned and strode off into the forest, *"Good luck!"* they yelled, *"Keep safe."*

"I'm free I'm free, whoopee I'm free." It hollered and roared with yellow eyes glowing in the moonlight, it was a frightening sight nine feet tall with long black hair and large feet.

They looked at each other trying to take in all that had happened.

Finally Oscar spoke, *"It will be light soon, I think we should get some rest before we make our way back to Astro3."*

Chapter 10

A Brave Decision

The next morning the team made its way back to the probe. The night had been cold so it was good to feel the warm sun as they moved quickly through the forest.

"Yesterday was an extraordinary day," said Oscar suddenly, *"and I think we've made a friend."* They nodded in agreement.

The trees eventually gave way to a clearing with long blue grass and sitting in the centre was *Astro3* gleaming in the sun. Looking back, Polly thought she saw a dark figure following them. Could it be the Pod, she wondered. They were soon on board with burners roaring, and within seconds the probe lifted off, with Red at the controls, heading back to their friends with an amazing story to tell.

There was great excitement as *Astro3* landed at base,

Captain Olive had a mountain of questions to ask. What had they discovered? Why did they stay in the forest overnight? Are they all OK?

"We need to talk urgently," interrupted Oscar, *"to consider all the discoveries we have made."*

Olive explained about the caves *Sky9* had seen the day before on the lower hills and how Noah had returned to take a closer look.

"We need them to return," ordered Captain Oscar, *"we have some serious decisions to make and they must be made this morning."*

While they waited Olive informed Oscar and his team what *Sky9* had discovered on their journey. The large caves, the bones and the unusual cone-shaped object. She finished her story but nobody spoke. Strange, she thought, I wonder what stories they have to tell.

Olive would not have to wait long because a roar of retro burners could be heard overhead and Kitty landed *Sky9* with hardly a bump.

Within minutes the crews of *Asterix1*, *Astro3* and *Sky9* were standing together listening to what Noah had discovered.

"We found digging tools scattered around the caves along with heavy silver rock, and at the back we found large bones probably from animals that had died there."

Oscar looked at Polly, and her head was bowed.

"We also found a silver ring, very heavy and forged by skilled life forms."

"We have a sample," interrupted Tom, as he lifted silvery blue rocks and a ring out of their probe.

"Be careful with the ring," shouted Red, *"we know all about them and the damage they can do."*

"Sit down," said Oscar, *"it's time we told you of our mission to the forest and the unbelievable discoveries we've made."*

He began with their journey through the dense forest and Polly's discovery of the ring hidden beneath a tree. It was a trap that Red had seen before. We were aware of the dangers but we carried on. He told of the awful wailing noise and the large animal with a ring clamped to its wrist, and how Polly had calmed it down with the intergalactic sign of peace and its understanding of Earthling.

Oscar then related the Drag Pod's story word for word and its warning about the Green Aliens. No one spoke, it was a truly astonishing tale. Red explained their difficulties with the Argon Key and Polly coming to the rescue and finally freeing the Drag Pod. There were many questions, some they answered and others they couldn't.

"I think this is a good planet to make our home," said

Oscar in almost a whisper. *"The air is pure with plenty of food and water resources. The ground is fertile to grow our crops. The gamma rays from the sun can provide the energy we need to charge our solar batteries. But, if we stay, eventually we would have to face the Aliens who will demand the Silver Rock. Perhaps we can trade with them but if they are aggressive we must be prepared to fight."*

Nobody spoke.

"Or, we could leave this planet and seek another home further into the Amber Moons that might not be of interest to the Aliens. "

He paused for a moment then continued.

"This is the momentous decision we have to make. Olive, you and Noah have the authority to decide for Moonlight, and Star Shine, speak with your teams and be back here as soon as possible with your answers."

Red, Polly and Oscar looked at each other, they were quiet and thoughtful. *"I want to stay,"* said Polly softly, *"Yes, me too,"* added Red loudly. Oscar smiled, it was the answer he hoped for.

Olive returned with her team followed by Noah. They had taken only a few minutes to decide.

"We want to make this our home," Olive said firmly.

"Yes, Star Shine the same," shouted Noah, *"and fight if we must."*

"Great, we all agree," said Oscar, *"because we also want to stay."*

There was a long group hug. It was a very brave decision but one they all shared.

When the three transporters were informed of what had been agreed there was great excitement mixed with concern about the possible Alien threat. Make your ships ready for landing was Captain Oscar's order, you will see your new home early tomorrow morning.

Chapter 11

Safe Landings

Noah and his team were sent to the fields near the lake to prepare the ground for the transporters to land. They would need a large area, flat enough and firm enough to take the size and weight of each spacecraft. The loose rocks and shrubs were cleared from the landing zone. Kitty had set up a string of lights and giro beacons of help navigation. Everything was now ready to welcome the transporters.

Olive was busy setting up a more permanent communications system while Ben and Holly marked out parking areas for the six space probes. Red and Polly were clearing a path from the lake to Base1, wide enough for a Moon Bug to travel through. There would be six of these trucks, two on each transporter.

Meanwhile Oscar was checking the flight calculations and weather for the descent through the gravity ring the next morning. He was leaving nothing to chance. *"This is Base1 and the landing site is Base2. Should we call the underground lake in the hills Base3?"* asked Olive.

"Yes," Oscar replied, *"Base3 will be a safe place for the children should they need emergency shelter."*

Cosmic Explorer with a large Z shining on its side was the first to attempt a flight into the gravity ring. It broke formation and glided toward, their new home. A slight shudder as it eased through the ring then, locating the giro beacons, it soon hovered above Base2 and with a blast of its retro rockets it was down. Good start, thought Oscar, just two to go. *Moonlight* with a large O on its side followed a similar course. It edged through the ring heading to Base 2 where it could see Z safely on the ground.

As it approached it shook a little.

"Rear Retro only half power," came the call from flight command, *"prepare for a difficult landing."* Passengers on O braced themselves. There was a heavy bump that rocked them in their seats then silence. *"Landing complete,"* came the message from the flight deck at last, *"slight damage to the rear stabilizer otherwise we are good."*

Star Shine was the last to enter the gravity ring, and it slipped through with hardly a shake. On the ground they all waved madly as the transporter with the large G on its side came into view. It hovered above them with burners roaring and completed a perfect landing.

The passengers and crew had arrived safely, they were eager to step outside, breath the fresh air and feel the warmth of the sun on their faces. Red and Ben stayed at Base1 while the two probes with Oscar, Polly, Kitty and Noah on board had flown to the landing site to welcome the transporters.

It had been agreed their leaders would be the nine who first landed on the moon. Together they would ensure a strong community was built, and crops were grown while exploration of the planet continued.

That evening plans were made to meet the most urgent needs of the community.

Medical facilities were already available on *Moonlight*, it had an advanced hospital unit with trained medics. This was a good start.

Children's education was considered next. *Cosmic Explorer* was the leaders choice as a safe place for them to meet and study. Polly was a Star Teacher, and she would organise all aspects of the children's learning.

The provision of food, water and energy was a major priority. Luckily Captain Noah was a skilled engineer and botanist. He needed temporary sheds near the lake for storage plus a lunar tent as a workshop.

Lunar tents were strong, they kept cool in the heat and warm in the cold. They required ten alongside each transporter, ten more in the fields and six at Base1. This would be a good start until stronger homes could be built. Red and Tom would oversee their construction.

Star Shine had an operational Science Lab on board that could analyse all the food samples gathered and test the water quality regularly. It would also study the Amber Moons and the star system surrounding them. Holly studied astrology, so she would be in charge. Kitty and Ben would map the planet by further exploration, while Olive and Captain Oscar would be responsible for security and communications.

Time passed quickly and it was easy to forget the Drag Pod's warning. Crops were already growing in the fields, children played happily and new buildings were appearing. Everyone was working hard and they were all proud of their achievements. The only thing still to be decided was a name for their moon.

Then one day Olive raised the alarm, a large space craft had appeared outside their gravity ring launching a small ship before moving away into the dark sky. Soon after, a green craft came gliding through the ring landing smoothly close to Base1.

Moments passed then a door slowly opened.

Chapter 12

A Dangerous Encounter

Captain Oscar, Red and Jed, the 1st engineer, were on their way to Base2 in a Moon Bug when the alarm call sounded. With a screech of brakes the Bug was thrown into reverse and thundered back the way it had come in a cloud of orange dust. They arrived back just as the doors of the green space craft were opening. Captain Olive, Polly and Ben stood in a line. Oscar and his team joined them.

Two beings in Green Lunar Suits appeared slowly looking around before stepping out into the sunlight. Are these the Aliens, thought Olive, they look similar to us but shorter. Oscar was thinking the same as he stepped forward giving the intergalactic sign of peace but the response this time was very different.

"We do not recognize your puny signs of peace," one boomed through his helmet, *"if you do what we say without resistance you will be allowed to carry on your miserable lives."*

Oscar was surprised how well they spoke earthling, just like the Drag Pod.

"We are free people," he said with a threat in his voice, *"if you wish to trade it is not a problem, we welcome you,"* but before he could finish the Alien roared in an even louder voice.

"Not a problem, not a problem! We are the Green Aliens. You do as we say, you give us what we want or we will destroy you without mercy as we did the Pods who lived here before you."

Polly smiled, *"Not all of them,"* she muttered.

"You think this amusing?" he raged, taking off his helmet and pointing at her. Oscar stepped in front of Polly fearing she might be in trouble.

Then Ben spoke up deflecting the Aliens, attention from both of them. He wondered loudly *"what the mighty Green Aliens would want on* a *small planet with no name."* It worked, they turned and stared at them with their eyes blazing.

"Do not insult our intelligence. We come here for a reason and you would be wise to remember it," the Alien snarled.

"Oh, could it be the Silver Rock you want?" Ben continued *"There is plenty if you wish to trade with us."*

"Behold the true face of an Alien Warrior" he said with an ugly smirk.

Olive was wondering what the Aliens would do next as they huddled together talking angrily. The second Alien stepped forward and said in a quieter voice.

"We are of superior intelligence with powers you cannot comprehend. We can quickly transform into the image of other beings and speak in their tounge so they understand our demands."

Then he boomed loudly. *"The Silver Rock is ours, we are the superior race. Do you understand."*

With that he bowed his head, placed his arms across his chest and started to hum. A few minutes passed before the humming stopped, then raising his head the Alien uncrossed his arms and took off his helmet. Captain

Oscar tried to keep calm but the others gave out a gasp of astonishment at what was now standing before them.

"*Behold the true face of a mighty Alien Warrior,*" he said with an ugly smirk.

The Alien's face was a dull yellow with grey lines, his eyes were green hollows with a red glow behind them and a round mouth showing a black wrinkled tongue. His head was now larger with no hair. This is not a pretty sight, thought Olive, as she got over the shock of seeing this sudden change. She couldn't see the feet but its hands were larger and arms longer.

"*Sago bog Alien tarp sago gross Alien troy,*" he bellowed. He threw his arms in the air, his red eyes glowing through the green hollows, his mouth wide open showing his long rough tongue. Oscar urged the others to move back because the Alien's face was full of anger. They did, except Ben who took a step closer and in a firm voice said.

"*I understand the Martian tongue, I was taught during the Martian Wars. You say Aliens own the rock and you will obey the Aliens or be destroyed.*"

Ben's intervention surprised them and it also surprised his friends. Polly stood open-mouthed but he had not finished.

"*We were driven from our planets and many good people were lost, we will not give up our freedom. We could be your friends but not your slaves.*"

With that he stepped back to join the others.

The Aliens were wild with rage. They had never been challenged like this before. Their faces turned red and Polly could see smoke coming from their ears as they spluttered threats that were indistinguishable even to Ben. Eventually they calmed down and strode back to their space craft. Standing on the top step they shouted.

"We will return soon, you must dig a cargo of Silver Rock ready for us to collect, if you do this we will not destroy you, YET."

The door closed and the Alien craft rose a few feet then, slowly turning, it directed its lazar cannon towards them.

"Down," shouted Red, *"it's going to fire."*

As they hit the ground a blast of flame shot over their heads, *"Missed,"* whispered Red. But it wasn't aimed at them. Looking back, the Moon Bug that Oscar and Jed had arrived in was now engulfed in flames.

As the smoke cleared the Aliens were gone.

"An abomination," said Oscar picking himself up, *"we have plenty to do if we are going to defeat these people."*

"Well there's no repairing the Moon Bug," said Jed with a weak smile, pointing to the blazing wreck behind them.

Chapter 13

A Tragic Event

When Oscar reported to the community there was a real sense of unease. However, there was also a real determination to fight for their home if they must.

The leaders would plan for the return of the Aliens but the work on the fields and buildings must continue. Holly flew Oscar back to Base1 and as their probe rose slowly above the transporters Holly gave out a cry.

"*Look, look,*" she said, "*a name for our moon right below us.*"

On the ground the transporters stood in a line, Cosmic Explorer first with a large Z on its side, Moonlight next with an O and finally Star Shine, G.

"*Wow! A name that includes us all, ZOG, planet ZOG. Well-spotted,*" said a delighted Captain Oscar, "*good work, Holly, we now have a name, ZOG."*

Everyone agreed ZOG was an excellent name. It was simple but included all the people from the three Alphabet Moons.

They all knew ZOG couldn't defeat the Aliens in battle with the weapons they had. Jed suggested it was possible to remove the rear cannon on the transporters and place them around the base to deter unwelcome visitors. They agreed, one would be placed at Base1, another in the fields close to Base2, and the third near the underground lake where the children would be sheltered.

This was a start but not enough to fight the Green Aliens. They needed another plan, but what?

As the days passed the space scanner was operating 24 hours a day. Children had reported seeing a black figure sitting in the trees watching them as they played. Casper, the youngest, said it had long hair and big feet. Kitty was Casper's guardian and she was also his absolute hero, a Star Space Pilot, as he reminded his friends every day. Polly had also spotted a moving shadow near Base1 just the other evening. Could it be the Drag Pod, she had wondered. Everyone worked hard but they were worried at the thought of another visit from the Aliens.

Then something did happen. The warning lights flashed, an incoming craft had been observed approaching their gravity ring. It glided through effortlessly and approached ZOG. Oscar and Olive watched the red lights on the scanner, unsure what to do, but before they could do anything a voice came out of the sub space radio.

"Permission to land, permission to land, we are from the Dark Moon and come in friendship."

Captain Oscar spoke in a commanding voice.

"We welcome all who come in peace. You have permission to land, please follow the landing beacons."

Olive switched on the landing beam then followed Oscar outside to see the incoming craft. Jed the chief engineer was already there as a white ship, twice the size of a space probe, came into view and hovered above zone 3.

The descent was almost silent. Then, without warning, it shuddered violently and veered sideways, smashing into a tree before falling to the ground with a mighty crash. They rushed to the wrecked craft. A side portal had broken open and looking in they could see two dazed passengers, Olive climbed inside and pulled one out followed by Oscar who carried out the other.

Smoke was now billowing from the wreck. *"Please, one more,"* said the last passenger desperately pointing to the craft.

"There's one more."

"Must be someone else still trapped inside," shouted Jed as he rushed back and climbed in.

Seconds passed and flames could be seen spreading to all parts of the wreck. Oscar ran to help Jed but a sudden flash followed by an almighty explosion blew them all to the ground. Polly was first up, she stared in disbelief at the raging fireball then dropping to her knees cried uncontrollably as their friend Jed was lost in the blazing inferno.

Oscar ran to help Jed but a sudden flash followed by an almighty explosion blew them all to the ground.

Help arrived and the fire was quickly extinguished. A tearful Polly, Oscar and the two passengers sat silently in the medical tent, heads bowed.

After a while Oscar stood up and spoke to the passengers.

"I am Captain Oscar. We welcome you to our moon. I am sorry we could not save your friend but we will give you all the help we can."

"My name is Corky," said their leader, *"and this is our pilot Tan. Our colleague who died in the fire was Tip. Thank you for saving us. We are saddened both Jed and Tip perished in the fire. I would like to use your communication station to contact our moon requesting another Space Beamer to pick us up. It will take a night to reach us. While we wait there's a lot we could discuss."*

Tom brought food and drink. They speak earthling and are very much like us, he thought. Tan told how a rear burner had misfired and, despite her efforts, threw the Beamer sideways and into a tree.

"I think we should rest for the night," said Oscar, *"it's been a tragic day, we can talk in the morning."*

Chapter 14

Visitors From The Dark Moon

The next morning Oscar found Corky looking at the burnt-out Beamer. They stood together for a while then Oscar spoke.

"Why have you come to our planet?" he asked.

"We have observed your arrival on this moon," Corky replied, *"we believe you are peaceful people who we can trade with and become friends. We have also seen the Aliens visit this moon. These are evil people, beware of them."*

They made their way to the control centre where Polly, Noah, Kitty and Tan were waiting.

Captain Oscar recounted their escape from the Weather Bomb, their journey to the Amber Moons and discoveries they hade made. Polly eagerly told of their adventure in the forest and the awful arrival of the Green Aliens.

"And we call our new home ZOG," shouted Olive, who was sitting at the scanner watching for any unusual activity outside their gravity ring.

Corky thought it a truly incredible story.

Then Tan spoke.

"But what defence do you have against the Aliens when they return?"

"Not much," came the worried reply.

"We can produce weapons but it will take time, we may have to obey the Aliens until we are ready to fight."

For a few moments there was silence then Kitty spoke.

"Corky, tell us about your moon and where in the cosmos it sits."

Corky told how their ancestors had discovered the Dark Moon many years ago, travelling through seven time warps before finally crash landing on its surface. Their planet was also part of the Amber Moons but they had developed a Black Magna Arc that kept them invisible from space. It blocked out the radar from other moons and space travellers such as the Green Aliens.

"It's kept us safe for many lunar years," Corky said quietly.

"We visit this planet once a year to collect fruit that we cannot grow on the Dark Moon, like hall apples and wild berries," he continued. *"These are healthy foods with medical and nutritious values, especially for children. I hope this can continue, we have many things to trade with you."*

"Yes," interrupted Tan, *"we have techno science that can help you battle the Aliens, like an Ultra Shield that can be erected quickly outside your gravity ring. It cannot stop Alien fighters passing through but any missiles fired from outside the ring explode as they touch the shield's force field and this keeps you safe from long-range attack."*

Corky reminded Tan they would need the approval of their leader, Yang, before this could happen, but if he agreed their *Wasp* fighters could be part of a trade deal.

"You are excellent flyers, I believe, and with a little training from Tan you would be superior to the Green Aliens. Their craft are well-armed but heavy and slow. I would like to talk to the Beamer that is on its way to collect us," he said, *"then we would like to meet more of your people."*

"Great news," shouted Corky as he ran from the control centre.

"There's a Beamer on the way and should be with us tomorrow morning. Our leader, Yang, is coming. He wishes to meet with you and thank you personally for saving us from the fire. It will be a good opportunity to discuss what

help we could give in your struggle with the Green Aliens."

"We have a lot in common," said Tan, *"I think a friendship deal would be good for us both."*

They all agreed.

The day passed quickly, Corky was impressed with the lines of fruit trees. When he last visited the fruit was difficult to get at, but now the long grass and brambles had been cut back with small paths running between. Beyond he could see fields of crops stretching right up to the slopes of the Blue Mountains.

"This is impressive," he said again.

Noah pointed to the channels of water they had cut in the rock that ran from the lakes in the mountain to all parts of the community providing fresh clear water.

Tan meanwhile had gone with Kitty and Ben to prepare a dock for the arrival of the Beamer. They talked about the *Wasp* fighters that only need a small area to land and take off.

"I think eight would be a good number to start with," Tan suggested.

Kitty was eager to know all about these fighters and she listened intently to what Tan had to say. A *Wasp* was smaller than a Probe but faster and easy to twist and turn in battle, with a small lazar cannon beneath each wing.

"I will train you," she said, *"but I think you will all learn very quickly."*

Meanwhile in the forest the Drag Pod continued its hopeless search for the Sacred Orb. The loud explosion yesterday had startled the creature, so it decided to make another trip to Base1 to be sure Polly was safe. The Drag Pod could see the camp from the tall trees close to the tents. It was something it had done many times before.

Chapter 15

Eight Wasps

A loud humming woke Red the next morning. He rushed outside just in time to see a Beamer in the landing zone. Captain Oscar, Olive, Kitty, Polly, Tan and Corky were shielding their eyes from the sun as the doors opened and a tall man with silver-grey hair appeared. He gave the sign of peace and moved down the steps, Corky greeted his leader and introduced Captain Oscar.

"*Must be Yang,*" whispered Holly who had joined the group.

Yang gave Oscar a warm embrace and thanked them all for saving Tan and Corky from an awful death.

"*They tell me we can be friends and help you with your fight against the Aliens with a mutual trading pact. Now please allow me time alone to talk with them.*"

While they talked Olive examined the Beamer. Two

hours passed until at last Tan reappeared.

"Come," she said, *"our leader has something to say."*

"As Leader of the Dark Moon I offer the hand of friendship and a trade deal with you the people of ZOG," Yang announced. *"As a sign of our goodwill I command an Ultra Shield be erected. Eight Wasp fighters will be delivered immediately in return for supplies of the Sun Rock."*

"You call it Silver," whispered Tan.

"We must now journey back to our home, but Tan will stay to train your flyers and help install the shield," he said with a wave.

Oscar and Olive spent a few minutes in the Beamer thanking Yang and saying goodbye to Corky. Then it slowly lifted off into the blue sky.

"I can't believe it," said Kitty, *"new friends to help us in our battle with the Aliens."*

"Well, lots of work to do before we can relax," Tan replied, *"but you are right, this really is a historic moment for both moons."*

The next few days passed quickly and sites were identified as bases to house the *Wasp* fighters. Lunar tents were erected for the pilots to sleep in with camouflage netting to conceal them. Noah, Polly, Kitty, Holly, Cat, Ben,

Joe and Oscar were the selected flyers, with Red as standby. They were all ace pilots. Tan was an excellent trainer and it was exciting listening to her.

Then it happened. A transporter was seen entering the gravity ring moving carefully to Base1 and landing with ease. They raced to see the *Wasps* and were not disappointed. Two were already unloaded and looked magnificent in the disappearing sunshine.

"*Wow*," said Joe, "*I can't wait to get flying.*"

"*Well, not today,*" answered Tan, "*let's rest. The real training starts tomorrow.*"

Chapter 16

Return of The Aliens

The next few days were fun. Tan was right, the nine flyers quickly learnt how to control the *Wasps,* Kitty was already flying upside down and doing loops. The children cheered the bright yellow craft as they swooped overhead. Tan had set up a firing range on a distant lake and with her expert help they all became deadly accurate.

"Remember," she said, *"your enemy will lose power as they come through the Shield. That's the best time to attack."*

Olive was astonished how quickly the Ultra Shield was erected. It was controlled by a triangle of Silver Rock beacons set in the Blue Mountain and powered by gamma rays from the sun. She thought it genius, and showed the others how it worked and what to do in an emergency.

Soon it was time for Tan to return home. A Beamer was due that morning to collect her, but as it touched down

The children cheered the bright yellow craft as they swooped over head.

the alarm sounded warning of an unidentified incoming craft. Tan told the crew to stay inside the Beamer and as she did a Green space craft came into view and landed on the other side of the Base near to the forest.

Here we go, thought Polly, as she stood next to Captain Oscar with Tan, Tom, Kitty, Noah, Holly and Ben behind. Two Aliens appeared in the open doorway. This time they were not in the form of earthlings but in their natural Alien state, a yellow head with grey lines, black wrinkled tongue and large green eye sockets.

"Not a pretty sight," Kitty whispered to Tan.

Before Oscar could speak, the first Alien demanded to

know where the cargo of Silver Rock was.

"Bring it quickly and load it onto our craft or you will be sorry," he sneered, stroking the lazar pistol on his belt.

"We told you we would be back," screamed the second Alien, *"you are nothing and we are supreme beings. Now, get the rock or perish where you stand."*

"These pieces are all we have," said Ben stepping forward and pointing to the rocks on the ground.

"Two, two. What, just two! You insult us," the Alien stormed.

Tan lay there dazed with the Alien standing over her, lazar in hand.

He kicked the rocks, his yellow face turning red with rage.

Then, before they could move, the other Alien strode forward and grabbed Polly by the hair, his pistol pointing at her head.

"This one first," he laughed.

Tan sprang forward to defend her.

"No, no," she shouted, trying to grab the pistol, but a green fist struck her forcefully in the back and she fell to the ground. She lay there dazed, with the Alien standing over her, lazar in hand. This was a truly terrifying situation. What could they possibly do?

Chapter 17

An Old Friend

They were in shock, unable to move. Then, without any warning, a large black figure stormed out of the forest and in an instant threw itself onto the two Aliens, knocking them violently to the ground. Their lazars were sent flying through the air. They tried to stand but a fearful roar and a handful of stones sent them scrambling back to their space craft. As the door closed, angry Alien voices could be heard shouting and cursing, they were wild with rage.

Ben and Oscar picked up Tan and supported her as they all dashed frantically to the edge of the forest.

"Jeepers did you see that," said Holly, *"what is it?"*

"That's our friend the Drag Pod," answered Polly, *"and what a brave friend it is."*

"This isn't over yet," warned Oscar.

The Alien craft slowly lifted off the ground with its burners blazing, as it gradually turned to aim its lazar cannon straight at them. But the Drag Pod knew what the Aliens were going to do. Picking up a Silver Rock it moved to the back of their craft and hurled it with great force into the rear burner.

Had it been any old rock it would have blasted straight back out, but this was Silver and the result was very different. A horrible grinding noise and black smoke came out of the burner. The craft shuddered, then lurched sideways straight toward the forest at increasing speed. A deafening explosion erupted as it smashed into the trees, an explosion that no Alien could possibly escape from.

The eight of them were shaken but unhurt.

"We must find the Drag Pod," said Polly as they made their way through the thick smoke.

Ben was the first out, *"Oh dear,"* he gasped, *"it's hurt, it needs our help."*

The Drag Pod raised its head as they knelt close by.

"Good, you are all safe," it said in a weak voice.

But the Pod was not so lucky. The fur on the right side of its body, from the shoulder to its foot, was gone leaving just bare burnt skin. The blast from the Alien craft had caught their friend as it threw the rock into its burner.

"Just carry me into the forest and leave me. You have a battle ahead that you must not lose," it whispered.

They carried the Drag Pod into the shade of the trees while Polly brought fresh water and orbs to make it comfortable. She gently bathed the burnt body in cool water. This looks like a serious injury, she thought. They knew the Pod was right. They must quickly prepare the community for battle.

Tan wanted to stay and fight, but Oscar insisted she return to the Dark Planet.

"Help us from there if you can," he said urgently.

Chapter 18

The Orb of Life

Before returning to the Beamer, Tan spoke gently to the Drag Pod and kissed its hand. She had persuaded Oscar to let Red accompany her to the Dark Planet and return with an advanced Ghost fighter that had superior weapons, and warp speed.

"With a Ghost," she said *"you can attack the Aliens beyond your gravity ring with greater fire power."*

Soon they were lifting off from Base1. The Beamer was capable of ultra sonic speeds that would reduce their journey time home.

"Keep safe," shouted Olive as they disappeared into the blue and orange sky.

Olive returned to the control centre making sure the Ultra Shield was set and working effectively, while Oscar summoned the *Wasp* pilots to Base. They were already on their way, having heard the explosion, except Cat who was travelling from Base3.

Soon they were all together listening carefully to Captain Oscar.

"Your orders to fly," he told them, *"will come from Captain Olive at the control centre who will decide who enters the battle zone. Do not take off until she has given the order. The Aliens will have greater numbers but we are superior flyers, with a fighter that is faster and can turn on a Luna Penny. Kitty is the flight leader, and we must pass any information we learn while in battle to her."*

Those were his instructions.

"Good luck.Now return to your Wasps and prepare for battle," he ordered loudly.

Tom stayed at the control centre with Olive, while Noah returned to Base2 and organised the medical facilities on the *Moonlight Explorer.* He made sure the children were safely transported to the underground lake in the Blue Mountains where there were supplies of water, food and bedding.

The three transporters and other key installations were covered in camouflage netting making them difficult to see if Alien fighters broke through their defences. Every member of the community had a role to play in defending

ZOG, all well-trained, all determined to win the battle ahead.

It was nearly dark as Polly collected fresh water and food from the control centre to take to the Drag Pod. Then, by chance, she spotted a cone with gold streaks sitting on a shelf behind Olive.

"Noah brought it back from his journey to the Blue Mountains," said Olive. *"Not sure what it is. They found it in a cave with large animal bones."*

Polly brushed off the dust and took a closer look.

"Goodness," she said in great surprise. *"I think, I think this might be the Drag Pod's lost Sacred Orb of Life. The Pod must see the Orb now."*

She ran to the forest, but the Pod was asleep, so she placed the food and Sacred Orb by its side. Polly hurried back to the centre. She knew all the lights would be turned off during darkness. However, had she looked back she might have seen the Sacred Orb glowing softly, giving off a blue haze that lit up the trees and surrounded their friend the Drag Pod.

Not everyone slept that evening, Olive and Oscar hovered over the radar all night watching for any Alien activity.

Chapter 19

The Battle Begins

The next morning the sky was unsettled with an orange tint in the east.

"Could be a storm brewing," Olive said as she continued to scan the radar screen.

During the night she had spotted a large object moving towards ZOG, stopping between them and the Dark Moon.

"It must be the size of ten transporters," Oscar said in a worried voice, *"almost certainly the Alien Mother Ship the Drag Pod warned us of, and it looks like it's preparing to launch an attack."*

Kitty's team of flyers were standing by their *Wasps* waiting for Olive to order them into battle, and that order was just seconds away.

"Three Alien craft have blasted off from the Mother Ship," Olive announced, *"and heading this way. Kitty, Joe, Ben and Holly, prepare for take-off."*

The Aliens got nearer.

"Go, go, go, you Wasps," Olive ordered, *"good luck, keep safe."*

As the fighters zoomed towards the gravity ring, three flashes could be seen.

"What was that?" said Joe.

"Looks like the Aliens are firing magna missiles at ZOG," answered Kitty, *"but The Ultra Shield is working and the missiles are exploding as they touch it."*

The Alien missile bomber circled and tried again, but the shield was well-made and again their missiles failed. Two of them flew straight at the shield and a spray of blue sparks seemed to surround them as they passed through. Quickly Kitty was on the attack with some neat twists and turns, so she was behind the first bomber firing both lazar cannon.

Kitty veered to the left as smoke cascaded from the bomber, allowing Joe to zoom in from behind and with two more bursts of cannon fire it exploded into a ball of flame. Kitty was onto the second Alien and this time no help was needed. Firing both cannon it spiralled away into space in a mass of flames. Olive's voice came over the *Wasp Wireless.*

Quickly Kitty was on the attack with some neat twists and turns she was behind the first Bomber firing both lazar cannon.

"Good work, there is no sign of the other Alien craft, you are clear to return to base."

Kitty reported back to Captain Oscar.

"I think we caught them by surprise," she said, *"they were not expecting their missiles to fail or to be attacked when they passed through the gravity ring. They will probably return with fighters better prepared and ready for battle."*

She informed the other flyers what they had learnt that morning.

"Do not let the enemy get behind your Wasp and always attack from the rear."

Polly, Cat, Noah and Oscar were now on standby awaiting the call that would send them into battle.

The call soon came.

"Prepare for take-off. Eight Alien fighters are heading our way," Olive said urgently.

There was a short silence then, *"Go, Wasps, go! Good luck, stay safe."*

The four fighters soared into the darkening sky in a tight formation, closely watching the Ultra Shield for any sign of an Alien entry. Blue sparks flashed as the first Alien craft burst through.

Polly broke formation, slipping in behind and firing her cannon, but as she did the fighter spun to the right, Polly had missed. But she continued the chase coming in at a lower angle where she couldn't be seen and this time two lunar bolts sent the invader crashing into space.

Three more Alien craft came through quickly chased by the *Wasps*. Oscar and Noah destroyed two of them with a burst of withering cannon fire, but Cat was having trouble trailing a very tricky Alien. As she continued the chase, four more Alien craft joined the battle. One, seeing Cat struggle, slipped in behind her. She managed to destroy the Alien she was pursuing, but before anyone could give a warning, she was blasted from the rear, and her *Wasp* twisted away in flames.

Polly knew this was no time for tears.

"Come on, concentrate," she yelled, *"let's make them pay. Remember to attack from the rear, take a lower angle, they cannot see you from there."*

In the following minutes the four remaining Alien craft were destroyed in a show of incredible flying skills and heroics.

"Excellent work," said a breathless Polly, *"come on, let's get back to base."*

There was great sadness at the loss of Cat, but they knew a greater battle lay ahead if ZOG was to survive. Polly reported back to Kitty.

"Flying at a lower angle," she said, *"blinded the Aliens giving the Wasps a few seconds advantage in battle. The other thing is the weather, the sky is getting darker, it looks like a storm is not far away."*

"Well done," said Oscar from the control centre, *"great flying."*

They all rested by their craft awaiting the next call to battle.

Things were quite for a while until late afternoon when Olive's voice sounded out the warning,

"Alien craft on their way, prepare all Wasps for take-off

except Joe."

Joe wasn't happy, he wanted to be in the fight, but at least one *Wasp* needed to be in reserve on the ground.

"*It looks like eighteen Alien fighters plus two missile carriers,*" she said, "*good luck all of you, keep safe, now go, Wasps, go.*"

It was a thrilling sight to see the six *Wasps* blast into the thunderous yellow sky. Polly was right, there was a big Solar Storm brewing, large enough and strong enough to destroy them if they got in its way. They must be careful.

Chapter 20

Outnumbered

As the *Wasps* reached the Gravity Ring, blue flashes could be seen as the Aliens eased through the Ultra Shield. It was getting darker with a strong wind. *"Pick your targets carefully,"* Kitty's voice ordered over the *Wasp Wireless*, *"if you spot the bombers let me know."*

Oscar was the first to break formation, quickly slipping in behind an enemy craft and blasting it with both cannon. Great start, Holly said to herself, as black smoke spewed from Oscar's target. Ben was busy pursuing another Alien craft with the same result, thick black smoke and flames sending it spiralling into space.

The whole team were now engaged in battle. Ten of the Alien craft had passed through the shield so far.

Kitty and Holly were fighting like demons. Their *Wasps* were zipping in and out of the enemy at great speed causing so much confusion two of the Aliens collided, both going down in flames. In just a short time they had destroyed four Alien craft. Polly showed great coolness when an Alien was on her tail. It was closing in for the kill, but as it did she performed a skilful loop manoeuvre that Tan had taught them. Within seconds she was behind her pursuer and wasted no time in blasting it with both cannon, a fantastic piece of flying.

Eight more Aliens had come through the Ultra Shield replacing those already destroyed. It would be a long battle. Ben was being chased by two craft, and Noah, seeing the danger, put his *Wasp* into a tight spin coming up beneath them before firing both cannon in quick succession, taking out the two Aliens in one attack.

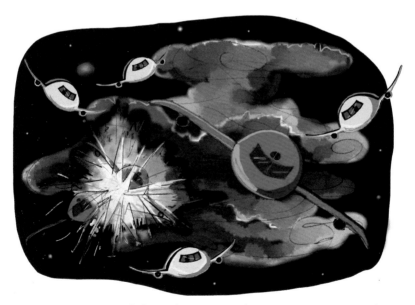

Kitty and Holly were fighting like demons their wasps zipping in and out of the enemy at great speed which caused so much confusion two of the Aliens collided both going down in flames.

Things were going well but then disaster struck.

Ben was caught in an Alien trap. A missile bomber came through the shield very slowly making it an easy target. He should have reported to Kitty, but seeing what looked like an easy kill he quickly flew in behind it. This was a deliberate ploy by the Green Aliens, as their second bomber sneaked through the shield unseen coming up behind the *Wasp* and firing a single missile into an unsuspecting Ben. There was a ball of flame as his craft exploded into a thousand pieces. He had been the victim of a fiendish trap.

Worse was to follow.

Noah was full of rage when the bombers dipped their wings celebrating Ben's destruction. In a flash he flew in between them releasing a salvo of deadly cannon fire at the leader, but before he could move away the second bomber had him in its sights and with a mega missile Captain Noah was obliterated.

Two *Wasps* had been lost in a few minutes. The team were in shock but they needed to focus on the other Alien fighters. They had been battling for nearly two hours destroying seven Aliens and one missile bomber, but just four *Wasps* remained. I wonder where Red is, Kitty thought to herself, we really could do with him now.

Holly was out for revenge, flying at full max speed between the enemy fighters before taking out two Alien craft with superb accuracy. Polly joined in the confusion, destroying a craft that seemed to be stalking a sluggish Oscar.

"I have a loss of power, I'm just 50 per cent at max," he shouted.

"Can you get back to base," Kitty asked anxiously.

"Yes, but I'm not leaving the battle," he replied, *"I will try to give you some protection from the rear, my lazar cannon are working okay."*

"The missile bomber and a fighter are moving away from the battle zone heading for ZOG," Kitty said with alarm. *"I must stop them or our community could be destroyed."*

Her *Wasp* spun away into the fierce wind. *"Good luck and watch out for the storm, it's getting very close,"* she warned.

Two of them were now facing seven green fighters with a damaged Oscar to protect if possible. They were outnumbered, it was a desperate situation and the storm was getting worse. The wind was so strong it was difficult to keep control of the *Wasps*.

The Aliens knew Oscar was lacking speed and tried to attack him, but Holly and Polly forced them away with some tricky moves. However, one did slip through and flew straight at him. He didn't move a whisker, he just shut his eyes counted to five and fired both cannon. When he opened them he could see a green space craft limping away, and his hands were shaking.

"That was close," he whispered.

One Alien fighter circled the Wasps. Were they planning a final attack?

"When they come at us don't worry about me," Oscar ordered, *"you two fight like wildcats, it's your only chance."*

The Aliens hesitated.

Then to everyone's surprise they moved towards the Ultra Shield and in seconds, with a shower of sparks, six Aliens had passed through. The last Alien craft, the one Oscar had damaged, was not so lucky. As it hit the shield its boosters closed down, it shook violently, broke in two and fell away into the stormy sky.

"Have they gone," said Polly. *"Why, what has happened?"*

"Be careful, they could be back at any time," warned Holly. *"We must call Olive, she will locate where they are."*

Olive confirmed the enemy were on their way back to the Mother Ship, *"You must all return to base, the solar storm is closing in,"* she said, *"the nearer you get to home the safer you will be."*

There was a long fizzing sound, then nothing. The communication system had gone dead.

Chapter 21

Attacking the Mother Ship

Four hours earlier, Red and Tan had arrived on the Dark Moon.

"*Any movement from the Mother Ship,*" Tan shouted to Corky, who was waiting at the landing port.

"*Three missile carriers were heading for ZOG this morning,*" he replied. "*Only one returned, so it looks like the Ultra Shield is working. Soon after, eight fighters were launched in battle mode, and as yet none of them have returned. The light isn't good and we have a big Solar Storm closing in.*"

Tan explained what had happened on ZOG.

"*I must speak to Yang. We need to launch a Ghost fighter. If he agrees, Red will fly with me.*"

"*What's your plan,*" Corky asked, "*Not sure yet,*" she said with a smile, *"but I'm working on it."*

Yang was concerned.

"Once again our friends have saved your life, so I agree you can launch a Ghost fighter," he said. *"But you, fighting the Aliens, could expose our planet to terrible danger. So I command you do not return to our planet until the Aliens are defeated or have departed from the Amber Moons."*

Tan nodded in agreement.

Their Ghost fighter was docked at Sky Port3, armed with a lazar cannon on each wing and two lazar missiles set under the flight deck.

Tan's Luna Watch bleeped.

"Eighteen Alien fighters and two missile carriers have been launched from the Mother Ship. It looks like a big battle," she said calmly.

They quickly slipped into Ghost3 and the flight deck control panel lit up. They were ready to go.

"We don't have the firepower to destroy the Mother Ship, and there is no time to return to ZOG, so this is my plan," Tan whispered. *"If we attack the booster engines on the Mother Ship, we might slow it down so it cannot escape this wild Solar Storm, hopefully making it impossible for them to launch more fighters. I think it's our best chance."*

"OK," said Red, *"let's do it."*

Their sleek white fighter glided out of the launch pad, with Red at the controls, into an eerie yellow and green sky. As they passed through the Black Magna they were buffeted by a fierce wind. This will test his flying skills, Tan said to herself. Her job was to seek the target and despatch the missiles.

"Three hours at max speed before contact," she said, *"their defence force field should be off, and the Aliens will not be expecting an attack. We will approach low from behind to target the rear boosters."*

As Red roared away, Kitty was in the sky above ZOG in a desperate fight to save their planet. Six *Wasp* fighters battling twenty Alien craft.

Chapter 22

The Solar Storm

Ghost3 approached unseen, the Mother Ship was enormous and completely painted in Alien green. Tan prepared to attack the large port booster. A space craft this size would need mega burners to move quickly, she thought.

The attack began with Tan locking onto the port burner then releasing a single missile. It was an excellent shot, a bullseye, right in the centre. Red spun away preparing for the next attack. There was a loud grinding noise but until the Aliens fired up the engines they wouldn't know what damage had been done.

"*Look out,*" shouted Tan, "*we've got company,*" she pointed to two green fighters above them.

"*OK, let's do battle,*" Red replied.

The wind was storm force but he was a top class flyer

with plenty of tricks. He slipped in behind one Alien allowing the other to get behind him. The Aliens thought they had him, but in a flash he did a double loop finishing behind his pursuer, giving it both lazar cannon before dodging its wreckage and blasting the other Alien in the same way.

Two destroyed in one attack, "*Superb flying, Red,*" said Tan smiling.

A Solar Storm could last for hours. It would begin with a ferocious wind that drove small rocks at great force through a wide corridor. As a storm grows the rocks become larger. Any space craft caught in this vortex would be in real danger and unlikely to escape unscathed.

Tan let out a scream.

"*The boosters on the Mother Ship are starting to fire. Quick, one more attack before we make our escape.*"

Once again Red zoomed in behind the Aliens ready to blast the starboard booster.

"*Here we go, keep steady Ghost3,*" he whispered.

Their last missile was on its way as the booster began to glow red.

"*Just in time,*" Tan said as it smashed into its target, dead centre as usual.

Red arched away at full max speed.

"We need to get to the edge of the storm double-quick" Tan yelled.

Small rocks were already rattling against their fighter.

"There are six Alien craft struggling to dock into the Mother Ship," Tan shouted, looking back, *"but it's lurching sideways, the boosters are misfiring, they look in trouble."*

Their last missile was on its way as the booster began to glow red "just in time" Tan said as it smashed into its target dead centre as usual.

It was a real shock when a large rock smashed against their windscreen, cracking it from side to side. It was a scary ride before they reached the safety of the storm's edge.

"We should plot a course under the storm to ZOG," said Tan.

But suddenly a soft glow lit up the horizon followed by a dull boom that sent shock waves through the sky, violently rocking Ghost3.

"Wow! Did you see that?" shouted Red, *"Must be the tail end of the Solar Storm blowing itself out."*

"Could it be the Mother Ship," said Tan hopefully.

"Mm, not likely," answered Red. *"I think it would take more than a storm to destroy the Alien monster we attacked. Come on, let's join our friends on Zog ... if they have survived the Aliens' onslaught,"* he added with concern.

Chapter 23

Kitty

Kitty was worried about leaving Holly, Oscar and Polly to battle the Aliens alone, but if the missile bomber managed to attack their community it could be the end of planet ZOG.

The bomber had a fighter for protection. This was a planned move by the Aliens, knowing only four *Wasps* were now active in the battle zone. The bomber was in range of Kitty's cannon, but the fighter kept moving between her and the target, preventing the *Wasp* from getting a clear view.

I need to get rid of him, she said to herself. In one sudden move, Kitty put her *Wasp* into a downward spiral then upwards at max speed straight at the Alien. One blast should do it, she thought, but to her horror there was no response from her cannon. She tried again, nothing, her guns had malfunctioned. Kitty managed to pull out of the attack, flying a wide arc above the Aliens to think what her next move should be.

She called Olive at Base1 to send up Joe without delay to attack the Alien fighter, in a few minutes the bomber would be near enough to unleash its missiles.

Joe was soon on his way, keen to be part of the battle at last.

He quickly spotted the three craft, one yellow *Wasp* behind two green Aliens. He was soon on the tail of the enemy fighter, but each time he tried to lock on his lazar cannon it would dive away or move under the bomber. This was a serious situation, and time was running out, so he made a risky decision to pursue the Alien under the bomber. As he did, the Alien sped away in front of the bomber, but this time Joe had his cannon locked on and sent lazar fire into the enemy fighter sending it spinning away in flames.

However, this was a dangerous move. He now found himself in front of the missile bomber, a bad position to be in, and before he could take evasive action a fiery bolt was on its way, destroying his *Wasp* instantly.

Kitty was horrified. Not only had they lost Joe, but the bomber was lining up to attack Base1. She called Olive to alert the gun crew of the incoming Alien attack, and in seconds they'd sent a salvo of canon fire at the enemy, but all wide of the target.

They never got a second chance. The Alien bomber fired a single missile at them blowing the whole unit to smithereens. Then, flying in a half circle, it prepared to attack the control centre.

What could Kitty do on her own with no firepower? But she did have a truly incredible plan in her head to save planet ZOG.

Chapter 24

An Incredible Plan

Olive and Tom watched in disbelief as Joe and the gun crew were both obliterated by the Aliens. Kitty was right behind the bomber as it now targeted the Control Centre.

"There must be something wrong," Tom said in alarm, *"she's not firing."*

Then it happened. Something you would not believe unless you were there to see it.

Kitty flew her *Wasp* under the port wing of the Alien bomber. Holding it steady, she blasted her booster engine sending her fighter straight up into the underside of the wing, making the bomber tip sideways. The Aliens struggled to control their craft but managed to straighten up, knocking down the communication beacon as it flew away in a tight circle.

"We have just watched the most sensational flying you will ever see," said Olive.

Tom agreed, *"But it's not over yet,"* he warned, *"it looks like they are preparing to attack the transporters at Base2."*

Tom was right, the Alien ship flew straight over Base1 lining up the three transporters that sat exposed by the lake.

But Kitty was not finished. She again shadowed the bomber, keeping out of their sight until it levelled up into an attacking position.

This time she slipped under the starboard wing, and keeping it steady she blasted her booster engine with the same result. The bump was enough to send the bomber lurching away from its target, but the Aliens soon wrestled back control and accelerated away across the lake.

Another superb heroic flying display, but her cockpit hood was badly cracked, and Kitty wondered if it would survive another collision. One thing she was sure of, the Aliens were not finished yet. The green bomber could just be seen far across the lake followed by a yellow dot. What would happen next, the people on the transporters were wondering.

Kitty knew the answer to that question, another attack on Base2 and this time they would be ready for any fancy tricks.

She sat in her battered *Wasp* closely following the Aliens. Olive had alerted the Lunar Cannon, situated in the fields close to the transporters, to fire if they could lock onto the bomber.

The Aliens knew the battle had not gone well, they were no match for the speedy *Wasp* fighters, but this was different, and a good opportunity to turn the tables on these inferior beings.

Only one damaged fighter to stop them.

They had lost contact with the Mother Ship but their orders were, "*the total destruction of these people,*" Orders issued from their High Commander must be obeyed.

At the far side of the lake Kitty was stalking the enemy. The sky was clearer, and the worst of the storm had passed but it was getting dark. Then the Aliens made their move, turning sharply over the water in line with the three transporters across the lake.

This is it, Kitty said to herself, as she accelerated after the bomber preparing once again to fly under its wing. But this time the Aliens were ready. They flew their craft so close to the water that it was impossible for a *Wasp* fighter to fly underneath without crashing into the lake.

This was a disaster, not only was her attack foiled but the bomber was flying so low the Lunar Cannon at Base2 couldn't lock onto it.

In seconds Kitty had hatched another plan just as daring, just as dangerous, only she could have thought of it so quickly. But would it work?

This time Kitty flew above the bomber, getting her *Wasp* in a position just over the port wing. She was so close she could see two Aliens sitting in the flight deck wildly pointing at her with long bony fingers.

"It's now or never," Kitty whispered. Then, closing her eyes tight, she shut down her boosters.

The *Wasp* immediately dropped onto the Alien's port wing forcing it into the lake with catastrophic results. The wing dragged in the lake sending the bomber into cartwheels across the water: one, two, three, four, five. Then it lifted high out of the lake before plunging down nose first.

It sank quickly with an enormous splash, a loud gurgling noise then silence, just bubbles floating on the surface. The Aliens were gone.

Kitty didn't see the bomber sink as she had her own problems. Her *Wasp* was struggling to gain height, it was only just above the water. She realised it was hopeless, so decided to try and land on the lake as near as possible to the Base. Kitty was a fantastic flyer but this was a truly impossible task even for her.

At first as she touched the water she skipped over the waves easily, but then her wing dug into the lake and, just

"It's now or never" Kitty whispered, then, closing her eyes tight, she shut
down her boosters. The Wasp immediately dropped onto the aliens port wing
forcing it into the lake with catastrophic results

like the Aliens, she went into a series of cartwheels finally
coming to rest floating upside down.

Slowly her fighter, disappeared below the water, she
was gone.

The tower at the Control Centre was broken, but Base2
could communicate with Tom and Olive, using a probe
transmitter. Tom was shocked when he heard the news, Olive
dropped to her knees hiding her face. Was Kitty really gone?

"Send out the boats to look for her," demanded Tom. *"We
already have boats on the lake searching,"* replied Base2,
"but it's getting very dark and difficult to see."

Chapter 25

Wasps Return

Back at Base1 their attention was taken by the sound of burners in the sky above them.

"Oh no," cried Olive, *"please, not more Aliens."*

It was dark, making it difficult to see but Tom, peering through the gloom, yelled.

"It's not an Alien craft. These are yellow and black fighters, they are Wasps and there's three of them."

Olive turned on the landing lights and within minutes the *Wasps* had safely touched down, the noise stopped and the dust settled.

Captain Oscar was the first to appear followed by Holly and Polly. Olive rushed to greet them hugging each one in turn.

"We were worried when we saw the cannon on fire and the control tower damaged. What happened?" asked Polly.

"No, please tell us your story first," urged Olive excitedly.

Almost whispering, Holly told of their battles, the loss of Noah and Ben, the shooting down of many Alien fighters, the bomber and a fighter heading towards ZOG with Kitty in pursuit.

"We were two Wasps at one hundred per cent, facing seven Alien craft, with a fierce storm raging," she said softly. "We waited for their next attack, but suddenly they disappeared through the Ultra Shield and were gone. Was it the storm or the Mother Ship calling them back, we don't know, but I'm sure they will return. We made our way home losing radio contact on the way."

Tom bit his lip, two more friends lost in battle and no news of Red. What next? he thought.

Then Olive spoke, telling how Kitty had stalked the bomber, but she had lost her firepower and she was flying without guns. Joe finally downed the fighter, but in doing so he was shot down.

"What happened next was a daring display of flying," she said proudly, "Tom, can you tell this part of the story please."

Tom hesitated then continued.

"Well, as the Alien bomber prepared to attack the Control Tower, Kitty flew under its wing, driving her Wasp upwards and making the Aliens wobble dangerously. They hit the communications beacon before heading towards the transporters at Base2, but Kitty repeated the trick sending them sideways across the lake."

Nobody spoke, Tom took a deep breath as this was the difficult part.

"Kitty destroyed the bomber over the water, but we don't know how. Base2 believe her Wasp was badly damaged and it disappeared into the lake. Our boats are still searching but it's dark and very cold, it's been too long, there's little hope of finding her now."

This was awful news. Polly and Holly stared at the ground while Oscar turned away to hide a tear.

Chapter 26

The Drag On

It was difficult to believe all this had taken place in just one day, friends lost in battle, so many brave deeds and still the Aliens were not defeated. They stood silently for a few minutes, the sky was black, the Amber Moon shone brightly, the Solar Storm had passed.

"Oh!" Polly said suddenly breaking the silence, *"the Drag Pod, we must find it."*

Olive grabbed some water while the others made their way to the edge of the forest where they had left their friend the previous evening sitting in the grass. Oscar shone his lunar torch between the trees but there was no sign of the Pod.

"I'm certain this was the place," said Olive, *"it must have moved deeper into the forest."*

"Wait," shouted Holly, *"there is a large black furry object*

next to this tree. It looks like a coat that has been burnt," she said holding it up.

Polly touched it, "*no doubt in my mind,*" she said softly, "*it belongs to the Drag Pod. But why is it here, what has happened?*"

Captain Oscar was deep in thought. He was trying to recall the conversation he had with the Drag Pod while they sat in the forest many weeks ago.

"*Yes, I remember,*" he said loudly, "*some of them evolve.*"

But his thoughts were disturbed by the sound of wings flapping and a bright light that moved between the trees.

"*Don't worry,*" he said calmly, seeing the frightened look on their faces.

"*I think I know what has happened.It's bravery has been rewarded and the Pod has evolved into a Drag On.*"

"*Yes,*" roared the Drag On as it landed close to them, still nine feet tall, and with golden wings and golden body it really was a magnificent sight.

"*I have evolved thanks to you, my friends. You saved me from the Aliens' trap and gave me the courage to act bravely. But above all these things you have found the Sacred Orb of Life and returned it to me. Without your help I would be nothing.*"

"I have awaited your return to thank you all before I follow the Drag Star and travel to our other world."

"But there is one last thing I ask of you."

Carefully it took the Sacred Orb from under its wing and handed it to Polly.

"I am the last Drag Pod on this planet. The Orbs work is done, but I believe, if it's kept safe, its mystic aura will keep the forest strong and allow all the plants and wildlife on this moon to flourish."

With that it kissed Polly on the head, touched the others on the shoulder, then with a mighty roar it flew upwards high above the forest.

They watched as its light gradually faded away in the night sky and was lost among the stars.

When they could see it no more they made their way back to Base silently, thinking of their remarkable friend the Drag On. Polly held the Sacred Orb tightly in both hands.

"We have the Aliens to worry about at the moment," she said quietly, *"but a safe home in the forest will be found."*

"We must repair the communications beacon urgently," said Olive loudly, *"we need to know who is entering our gravity ring. Now the storm has passed the Aliens will be back."*

Chapter 27

The Great Escape

Olive was up early the next morning eager to examine what damage had been done to the communications beacon. She was soon joined by the others.

"What do you think," asked Holly.

"Well, it's not too bad, if we rebuild the structure and rewire into the control centre, it should be OK. Probably a day's work."

But before she could finish they became aware of a low humming noise that gradually got louder. Looking up, a sleek white space craft came into view and hovered above them.

"What is it?" Polly asked grabbing Tom's arm.

"No idea, he said, but it's been in a battle, there are bumps and scratches all over it."

Oscar strode forward.

"Don't worry," he shouted pointing at the logo on the wings, *"it's from the Dark Planet."*

Within a few minutes the craft had landed, the door raised and to their amazement Red stepped out followed by Tan. The five of them cheered, it was an unexpected return but one that was very welcome.

"We were worried we couldn't communicate with you as we passed through the gravity ring," said Tan, *"but I can see your beacon is down. What happened?"*

"A lot in a short time," replied Holly.

She told of their battles with the enemy and Tom recounted Kitty chasing the Alien bomber, with no guns, eventually destroying it over the lake yesterday evening.

After a short pause he added.

"But her Wasp crashed into the water without trace."

Their smiles disappeared, Red closed his eyes, another victim of this terrible battle, he thought.

"What about you," Tom asked breaking the silence. *"Looking at your fighter, you two have been in a battle yourselves."*

Tan smiled.

"Yes, we have, but most of the damage was done by the violent Solar Storm."

"Our adventure began when Yang agreed we could mobilise one Ghost fighter. We knew the Alien bombers were attacking you, and our plan was to weaken the Mother Ship before it could launch any more green fighters."

Then, before Tan could continue, a Moon Bug, engine revving furiously, drove at great speed into the base, skidding to a halt in front of the Control Centre and creating a large ball of orange dust.

As the dust settled a figure could be seen standing next to the Moon Bug.

"No, it can't be," said Oscar, struggling to clear the dust from his eyes, *"it can't be."*

"Yes it is," shouted Polly as she ran forward, flinging her arms around the bedraggled figure.

"It's Kitty, she's safe."

They rushed forward surrounding Kitty and hugging her in turn.

"Stop," she said, *"it's hurting, I am covered in cuts and bruises."*

Stepping back, they could see her face was badly scratched with a nasty cut above her eye, the blood had congealed in her hair and her space uniform was in tatters. Seeing their shocked faces, she explained what had happened to her after the bomber had been destroyed.

"My Wasp was too close to the lake. I tried to land on it but my wing dipped into the waves sending me spinning across the water. We finished upside down and slowly sank."

"I was dazed but luckily as the Wasp sank the cold water hit my face bringing me to my senses. I kicked out the damaged screen and swam to the surface."

"It was dark and the lights at Base2 had been turned off during the attack so I swam to where I thought the base was, but in my confusion I swam the wrong way. I was dizzy and ached all over."

"When I finally got to the shore I collapsed under a tree."

"The next thing I knew the sun was shining on my face and I could hear a Moon Bug by the side of the lake. Bella from Base2 was searching for any wreckage. She saw me waving madly and immediately swung the Bug around and picked me up."

"On the way back we heard, over the wireless, an unidentified fighter had landed here. The only way to communicate with Olive was by using the Moon Bug radio

As the dust settled a figure could be seen standing next to the Moon Bug.
"It can't be" said Oscar struggling to clear the dust from his eyes. "It can't be."

but nobody was answering. Bella jumped out near the
Cosmic Explorer, then with full power I drove here as fast as
the Bug would travel, but I was worried what I might find
when I arrived."

"I must let our people know what is happening," said
Olive,"I will speak to them now, they will be delighted that
Kitty is safe and the White fighter was flown here by Tan
and Red."

"Yes, after yesterday's news it will give everyone a boost,"
added Polly.

"We must get on with the repair of the beacon," Olive

reminded them.

"With the storm gone the Aliens could be back at any time."

Holly had quietly explained to Kitty that six Alien craft had escaped to the Mother Ship, probably to shelter from the Solar Storm. Kitty thought for a moment then turned to Tan.

"We have just two combat-ready Wasps. The third one has a loss of power. Can it be fixed?" she pleaded, *"it sounds as if we will need it soon."*

"Yes," Tan replied, *"but before you speak to your people you should all listen to our story, the story we started just before you arrived, Kitty."*

Chapter 28

Unexpected News

What was so urgent, Oscar wondered, but he could see by the look on Red's face it was big news.

Tan started again, telling of their plan to damage the Alien Mother Ship, to slow it down and stop other Alien fighters leaving to attack ZOG.

"*This is Ghost3,*" she said pointing to the damaged White fighter behind her.

She described their attack on the Mother Ship, and the battle with two Alien fighters while struggling with the deadly solar storm.

"*The storm was so fierce,*" she said, "*large rocks were striking Ghost3 finally driving us away, but looking back I could see six Alien fighters trying to dock into the Mother Ship.*"

"The six that retreated from the battle zone," Polly muttered.

Tan continued.

"Well, we managed to get to the edge of the storm in one piece but as we did a massive flash lit up the dark sky followed by shock waves that rocked our craft."

"What was it?" Holly asked with a stutter in her voice.

"Was it, was it the Aliens, were they destroyed?"

There was silence before Red spoke again.

"We thought it might be the storm blowing itself out. The Mother Ship was so enormous and strong we didn't think a Solar Storm could actually destroy it. We had promised Yang we would not return to the Dark Planet unless the Green Aliens had gone or were beaten, so we decided to plot a course under the storm to ZOG."

"So the Aliens have survived the storm," said Polly, *"they could be back at any time."*

"Well, hang on a minute," said Tan, *"let Red finish."*

Red continued.

"We followed the course we had set under the storm. It was a rough ride and we were buffeted by strong winds.

Rocks rattled against Ghost3 but then we became aware something different was hitting us."

"What we could hear was a clanging noise as if metal was striking our fighter. Looking out we could see large pieces falling out of the storm being blown about like paper in the strong wind."

"It was Red's skilful flying that stopped Ghost3 being smashed to pieces by these metal objects," interrupted Tan.

"He ducked, dived, twisted and turned until we were clear of the danger."

"It was a truly terrifying experience," continued Red, "but we came through it smiling because those large metal objects we had flown through were green, not just any green but Alien green."

"Incredible as it sounds, the Solar Storm really had destroyed the Alien Mother Ship and its remains are now scattered across the far reaches of space."

Chapter 29

Victory

Captain Oscar fell to his knees. Could this be true? The Aliens beaten, the Mother Ship destroyed, the words were buzzing around his head.

Then Oscar spoke, but he had to shout loudly to be heard over the excited chatter.

"Listen," he said, *"listen."*

"Our fighters defeated many Alien craft but six escaped to the Mother Ship. We know because Tan saw them return. The fierce Solar Storm, with the help of Tan and Red, has destroyed the Mother Ship. No one could survive such a massive explosion. Then yesterday evening, Kitty sank the last Alien bomber over the lake."

Cheering, laughing and shouting erupted. Kitty was jumping in the air with Tan pretending to be *Wasp* fighters.

Tom cried in delight while the others enjoyed a very long group hug.

"This is incredible news," Oscar yelled, *"but before we start celebrating let's not forget our brave friends who we've lost in battle."*

"Yes, I agree," said Holly, *"we must have a day when we remember the many heroic deeds we have witnessed and on the same day celebrate our victory."*

There was another loud cheer.

"OK, it seems we all agree," said Oscar.

"I think it could be in three days, that will give us time to prepare for a very memorable occasion. Now Olive, I think you should inform the community of this momentous news and what good news it is."

"Well," said Tan after they had all calmed down.

"I must return to my planet and report to Yang, but I will be back in three days to take part in your celebrations."

"Bring Corky with you," shouted Oscar.

It was a short visit but, wow, what unbelievable news Tan and Red had brought with them.

As Tan entered Ghost3 she turned on the top step and

shouted back.

"It's about time you had your own flag. See if you can design one before I return. A flag that represents, all the people of ZOG."

The door slammed shut, and a burst of rocket slowly lifted her high above them. The Ghost certainly looked a mess with so much damage. Another blast shook the ground as Tan glided smoothly away quickly picking up speed and disappearing into the afternoon sky.

Olive rejoined the group.

Her news had been greeted with great excitement and relief that the fighting was over. They could now continue their work building the community of ZOG without fear of the Green Aliens returning.

Chapter 30

The Flag

"We have a lot of work in front of us," urged Captain Oscar.

"We must restore the communication link and test the Ultra Shield."

"Let's not forget the flag," Holly reminded him.

Oscar nodded, *"Any ideas then,"* he asked looking at each of them in turn.

There was silence, then Red suggested a *Wasp* fighter, or an Amber Moon, added Kitty.

Then Polly stepped forward speaking softly but clearly.

"There is one important piece of this story we have forgotten and that is our friend the Drag Pod. It saved our lives putting itself in great danger. Without it's bravery we would not be

here today celebrating a victory. I think a gold flag with a Black Drag Pod in its centre would be a tribute to it and the many other Pods who lived on this planet before us."

"It would also remind us of our epic battles with the Green Aliens."

Oscar beamed, *"What a fabulous idea,"* he said, *"simple but effective, what a stunning flag that would be."*

"Yes, Yes, Yes," they all screamed at the top of their voices.

"Drag Pod, Drag Pod, Drag Pod," they roared.

"OK," Oscar interrupted, *"OK, a Drag Pod it is."*

"Polly, it's your idea, you should speak with the other leaders. If they agree you are in charge of making sure the flags are produced in time for the celebrations. Now everyone, we have work to do before it gets dark."

That evening Olive was sitting on the steps of a Moon Bug observing the distant planets that were illuminated by the glow of the Amber Moon.

"What are you thinking," said Oscar as he stepped out of the Control Centre.

Olive stood up and pointed to the Amber Moon.

"Well, I was wondering if there is life on any of the other

stars," she said softly. *"The Dark Planet observed our arrival, so did others, were our battles with the Aliens seen?"*

Oscar was deep in thought then replied.

"That's a lot to think about Olive and I hope one day we will find the answers to those questions. But for now we still have large areas of this moon to be mapped and explored. We must also continue our work building a thriving community while Holly, and her team of scientists, study the Moons that surround us."

Oscar was silent, then quietly he added.

Olive stood up and pointed to the Amber Moon. "Well I was wondering if there is llife on any of the other stars " she said softly.

"And one day we must return to the Alphabet Moons to discover their fate."

"It's cold," he said with a shiver, *"I'm going back inside."*

Olive followed him up the steps. Stopping at the top she gazed once more at the Amber Moon.

"Keep shinning on us," she whispered.

Then with a smile she turned and disappeared into the warmth of the Control Centre.

Chapter 31

The Legends of ZOG

There are many moons in our universe. Some have intelligent life while others wait to be discovered. Those who embark on space exploration and make distant stars their home are true pioneers of our age.

As time passed ZOG prospered, its citizens were happy and welcomed many peaceful travellers. The news of their epic battles with the evil Aliens soon passed from moon to moon. Their exploits would, in time, be recorded in the annals of space travel.

It will be written.

"When the Alphabet Planets were destroyed by a Weather Bomb those who escaped journeyed to the Amber Moons, a little known constellation of stars deep in space."

"They settled on a small, uninhabited moon to build a

new community. However, to survive the brave people of ZOG had to face and defeat the feared Green Aliens. These were ruthless space pirates who had, for many lunar moons, terrorised the smaller stars. These cruel beings fought, stole and bullied without mercy."

"But defeated they were."

The saga of ZOG will soon be legend, a story retold time and time again across the Many Moons of the Universe. These fearless people are destined to become.

The Legends of ZOG.

Character Library

Captain Oscar Captain Olive Captain Noah

Kitty Red Polly

Drag Pod Alien Warrior

Ben Holly Tom

Jed Cat Joe

Tan Corky Yang